Why Johnny Doesn't Flap

NT is OK!

Clay Morton & Gail Morton
Illustrated by Alex Merry

...ca Kingsley *Publishers*
...don and Philadelphia

First published in 2016
by Jessica Kingsley Publishers
73 Collier Street
London N1 9BE, UK
and
400 Market Street, Suite 400
Philadelphia, PA 19106, USA

www.jkp.com

Library of Congress Cataloging in Publication Data
A CIP catalog record for this book is available from the Library of Congress

British Library Cataloguing in Publication Data
A CIP catalogue record for this book is available from the British Library

ISBN 978 1 84905 721 9
eISBN 978 1 78450 190 7

Printed and bound in China

This is my friend Johnny.

We have a lot of fun together, but sometimes he acts pretty strangely.

Mom says it is because he is NT, or neurotypical. He doesn't have autism, so his brain works differently from mine,

but that's OK.

Johnny is supposed to come to my house at 4:00, but sometimes he comes at 3:58 or 4:03. I gave him a watch for his birthday to help him arrive on time, but he still has this problem.

He may be hopeless when it comes to punctuality, but we still get to spend time together and have fun,

so that's OK.

When he comes into the house, sometimes he wants to play checkers first and then play crazy eights. Sometimes he wants to play crazy eights first. He doesn't know to follow the same order every time.

But we still get to play all our favorite games,

so that's OK.

When he talks to you, Johnny looks directly into your eyes, which can make you pretty uncomfortable. He doesn't mean any harm, though. That's just the way he is,

and that's OK.

Johnny watches the same
television shows that I do, but
he never recites the opening
credits word for word.

In fact, I'm not even sure he has
them memorized. He sure picks
funny things to focus on,

but that's OK.

When something exciting happens, Johnny doesn't respond like you would expect. He doesn't flap his arms or jump up and down. He just moves the sides of his mouth up and slightly widens his eyes.

Maybe he doesn't know
much about how to
express emotions,

but that's OK.

Johnny doesn't have a topic that he knows everything about, like World War II or dinosaurs or hydraulic forklifts.

I try to share in-depth information with him, but he seems uninterested.

He may never be a real expert at anything, but he is a good person,

so that's OK.

Johnny functions very well at school. He understands the rules and gets all of his work done.

But if you ask him for basic information about the school building—like what companies manufactured the elevator, intercom, and security system—he will stare at you blankly. He understands some things but has trouble with other things.

That's true
of all of us,

and that's OK.

Johnny never has a meltdown when disasters happen, like a fire drill or art class being canceled. He is afraid of what people might think. It seems like he is bottling his feelings up, but he just has his own way of dealing with things,

ART
CLASS
CANCELED
TODAY

and that's OK.

Johnny has problems with communication. He will say that a math test was "a piece of cake" when he really means that it was easy. I try to explain to him that cake has nothing to do with an easy math test, but he never seems to understand that he should say what he means.

On the playground Johnny always wants to play with other kids. He never goes off into his own world.

Sometimes I wonder if he ever gets a chance to sit and think about his favorite commercials or the recorded message on the subway. Maybe he's a little too obsessed with social interaction,

but that's OK.

It can be pretty interesting being friends with a kid who is NT. He has a lot of quirks that can be very frustrating until you get used to them.

Mom says that everyone's brain is different,
and different isn't always wrong.

I like Johnny. I think that being NT is OK.

A Note for Parents

Johnny, the character in this book, is a neurotypical, or NT, child. What does this mean? Neurotypical children lack most or all characteristics of autism. Like Johnny, they are overly flexible in their routines (if they even have a routine) and have a strong need to socialize with other people. They speak in nonsensical idioms, do not have obsessive interests, and almost never engage in stimming. "That's very interesting," you may say, "but what does that have to do with my child?" According to the Centers for Disease Control and Prevention, as many as 67 in 68 children may be neurotypical. So if your child does not currently have an NT kid in their life, they almost certainly will at some point. And what will this be like when it happens? Children with autism often find it very difficult to interact with NTs. Their chattiness, unpredictability, and bizarre ways of thinking can be bewildering and irritating. But it is important for autistic young people to understand that NTs are people too, and the fact that they are different doesn't mean that there is anything wrong with them.

In this book, we see that the narrator has problems relating to Johnny. He is never exactly on time, varies his rituals, looks directly into people's eyes, never has meltdowns, speaks cryptically, and never gets lost in his own world. But the narrator still likes Johnny, in spite of these quirks. He has a lot of fun with Johnny—and, as strange as it may sound, it's possible that he can even learn a thing or two from Johnny's unique perspective! As you read this book with your child, ask them if they ever observe these kinds of behaviors in other children. Talk about what they should do when certain awkward situations arise with an NT child. Above all, help them to understand that the differences between people make life interesting, and that being NT is OK!

About the Authors and Illustrator

Clay Morton is Associate Professor of English and Director of the Honors Program at Middle Georgia State University. **Gail Morton** (MLIS) is a Public Services Librarian at Mercer University. Clay and Gail research issues of neurodiversity, particularly in relation to higher education. They are parents to a child with autism and are both advocates for the neurodiversity movement. They dedicate this book to J.M.

Alex Merry is an illustrator and portrait painter from Stroud in Gloucestershire. Her eye for the quirky and love of human difference inform her artwork.